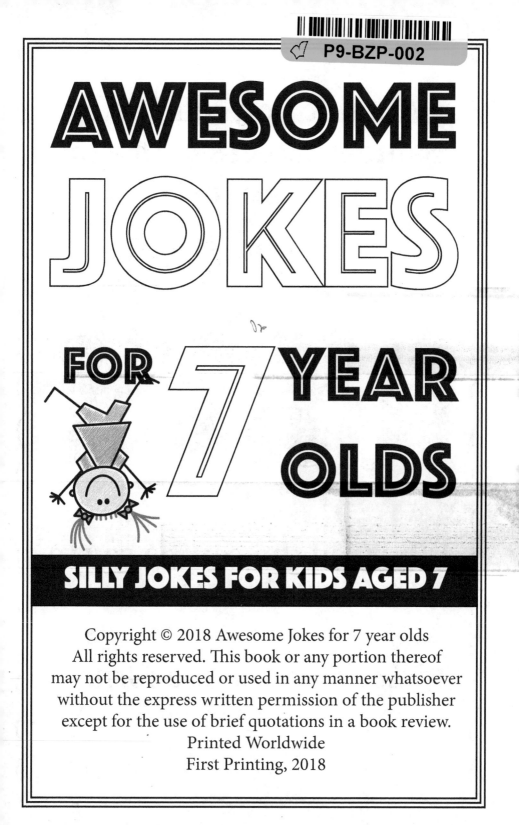

AWESOME JOKES FOR 7 YEAR OLDS

SILLY JOKES FOR KIDS AGED 7

What do you call one of Santa's helpers with a lot of money?

a. Welfy.

What did the ceiling say to the wall?

a. Let's meet in the corner.

Why did the shark cross the ocean?

a. To get to the other tide.

Knock knock.
a. Who's there?
b. Nana.
c. Nana who?
**d. Nana your business
who it is!**

What starts with P, ends in E, and has a ton of letters?

a. Post office.

What is a frog's favorite Apple device?

a. The lill-iPad

Knock knock.

a. Who's there?

b. Uncle.

c. Uncle who?

d. Knock knock.

e. Who's there?

f. Uncle.

g. Uncle who?

h. Knock knock.

i. Who's there?

j. Uncle.

k. Uncle who?

l. Knock knock.

m. Who's there?

n. Aunt.

o. Aunt who?

p. Aunt you glad I didn't say uncle?

Mother: Son, why are you standing outside with your umbrella upside-down?

Son: I'm collecting money!

Mother: Why on Earth would you think money would fall from the sky?

Son: The news said there would be a change in the weather.

Knock knock.
a. Who's there?
b. Atch.
c. Atch who?
d. Gesundheit!

Why do some cows have bells around their necks?

a. Because their horns don't make any sound!

Knock knock.
a. Who's there?
b. Who.
c. Who who?
d. Are you an owl?

What's a phantom's favorite ride?

a. A rollerghoster!

Which is slower, hot or cold?

a. Cold is slower, because you can catch a cold.

What do you call Dracula when he sleeps in a tent?

a. A campire!

What is a duck's favorite snack?

a. Quackers and cheese.

What is a mouse's favorite kind of joke?

a. Cheesy ones.

What type of melon is best at swimming?

a. Watermelon.

Why did the man wear two shirts when he went golfing?

a. In case he got a hole-in-one.

Who do frogs call when they need a secret agent?

a. James Pond.

What do shark magicians say?

a. "Pick a cod, any cod."

Why did the cabbage look away?

a. Because it saw the salad dressing.

Why did the cake go to the hospital?

a. It was feeling crumby.

How do you contact someone in prison?

a. Call them on their cellphone.

What does Santa teach to his young helpers?

a. The elf-abet.

What is a tree's favorite soda?

a. Root beer.

What do you call a helpful lemon?

a. Lemonaid.

What did the kindergartener's fingers say to the kindergartener?

a. "You can count on me!"

What did the buffalo say when his son left for college?

a. Bison.

What's something that everyone has that they can't get rid of?

a. A shadow.

What's salty and goes to outer space?

a. A rocket chip.

Why did the banana go to see the doctor?

a. He wasn't peeling very good.

Why don't lobsters share with others?

a. Because they're shellfish.

What has thousands of ears but cannot hear?

a. A cornfield.

What do you call a pumpkin crossed with a pirate?

a. Patches.

What doesn't ask questions but often gets answered?

a. A telephone.

What kind of button doesn't get sewed into clothes?

a. A bellybutton.

What did the table say to the chair?

a. Dinner is on me!

Why should you not try to fix a broken pencil?

a. Because it's pointless.

Why did the girl try to put a candle on her homework?

a. Because someone told her it was a piece of cake.

What did the father pickle say to his whiny son?

a. Dill with it.

What did the leopard say after her massage?

a. "That hit the spot."

When should you avoid a black cat?

a. When you're a mouse.

What do snakes study in school?

a. Hisstory.

What did the vampire say when he boarded his flight at the last minute?

a. Just in tomb.

How do you help an astronaut's baby fall asleep?

a. You rocket.

How do you make a lemon drop?

a. You just push it.

What did the limestone say to her boyfriend?

a. Please don't take me for granite.

Why are ducks so good with money?

a. Because they have bills.

What is it called when cows lead an uprising?

a. Udder chaos.

Why do seagulls always live near the sea?

a. Because if they lived near to the bay they'd be called bagels.

Why was the teacher wearing sunglasses in her classroom?

a. Because she had such bright students.

What is the best tree to slap?

a. A palm tree.

Why was the strawberry late?

a. Because it was in a jam.

Who is married to mom corn?

a. Pop corn.

Why did the bicycle go home early?

a. Because it was two-tired.

How much did the pirate charge to pierce ears?

a. A buccaneer.

What building in each city has the most stories?

a. The library.

What is a cyclone's favorite game?

a. Twister.

What will fall in the winter but can't get hurt?

a. Snow.

What does the ghost call his sweetheart?

a. His ghoulfriend.

What animal is the best at baseball?

a. A bat.

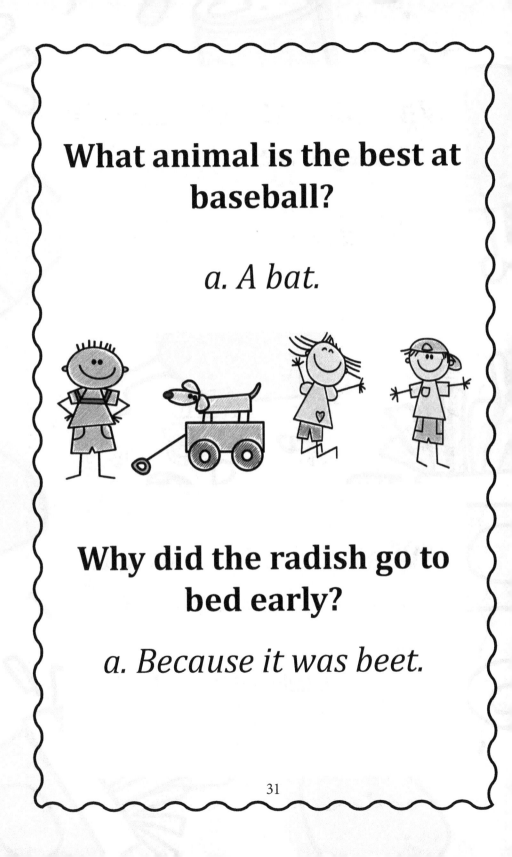

Why did the radish go to bed early?

a. Because it was beet.

Why does Albert Einstein always wear Denim?

a. Because he's a jean-ius.

What is the best way to talk to an elephant?

a. You use big words.

Why did the toilet roll go down the stairs?

a. To get to the bottom.

How does the moon clip the astronaut's hair?

a. Eclipse it.

Why did the grandpa give the computer medicine?

a. Because it had a virus.

How are earrings like the stars?

a. Because they come out at night.

What is the best circus performer to invite to Thanksgiving?

a. A tra-peas artist.

What kind of instrument will you find in your bathroom?

a. A tuba toothpaste.

How did the vampire know that he was sick?

a. Because he started coffin.

What kind of makeup should you have during Armageddon?

a. Apocalipstick.

What kind of lion isn't scary?

a. A dandelion.

What did the tooth say to the toothpick?

a. Quit picking on me.

Why did the girl take a parachute to school?

a. Because she was starting high school.

What does Dracula put in his fruit salad?

a. Blood oranges.

What runs around your yard but stands still?

a. Your fence.

What did the magician say when he was making the dog disappear?

a. "Abracalabrador."

Why did the skeleton stay at home on Valentine's Day?

a. Because it had no body to dance with.

What never leaves the corner but can travel anywhere in the world?

a. A stamp.

What gets wetter
as it dries?

a. A towel.

What gets broken
but cannot be fixed?

a. A promise.

A sailor docks on Sunday, stays for four days, then leaves on Sunday. How is that possible?

a. The name of his boat is Sunday.

What do you give a pumpkin that loses an eye?

a. A pumpkin patch.

What has a T at the beginning, T inside it, and a T at the end?

a. A teapot.

What kind of award do you give a bad dentist?

a. A plaque.

What kind of bed doesn't have pillows?

a. A flower bed.

Why are windows such terrible liars?

a. Because you can see right through them.

What did the bee say to the flower?

a. "Hey, bud!"

What do you call an old snow man?

a. Water.

What did the painting say when it was arrested?

a. "I was framed!"

When is a door no longer a door?

a. When it is a jar.

Where do astronaut bees go after they get married?

a. On their honeymoon.

What do you call a duck crossed with an almond?

a. A nutquacker.

When does December come before July?

a. In the dictionary.

What did the lawyer take to the dry cleaner?

a. Her lawsuit.

What time is it when a meteor hits your roof?

a. Time to fix the roof.

Why did the man bake a calendar into his cake?

a. Because the recipe said to add dates.

CPSIA information can be obtained
at www.ICGtesting.com
Printed in the USA
LVHW080518060520
655095LV00012B/2345